The Kingdom of Dreams

John Whitehead

Matador
9 Priory Business Park,
Wistow Road, Kibworth Beauchamp,
Leicestershire. LE8 0RX
Tel: (+44) 116 279 2299
Fax: (+44) 116 279 2277
Email: books@troubador.co.uk
Web: www.troubador.co.uk/matador

ISBN 978 1780881 508

British Library Cataloguing in Publication Data.
A catalogue record for this book is available from the British Library.

Typeset in 12pt Bookman Old Style by Troubador Publishing Ltd, Leicester, UK

Matador is an imprint of Troubador Publishing Ltd

For Diane Murray

Once upon a time there were two young children called Paul and Tess. They lived next door to one another; but they did not live in a street in a big city as you might suppose. In fact their homes were the only buildings of any kind for miles and miles around, and no one knew who built them, they were so very old.

The two houses stood side by side close to the edge of a pine-forest in a country whose name the teller of this story has forgotten. Paul and Tess were the only two children in that place, and for all they knew, in the whole world. They played together on the edge of the forest (they were forbidden to go into it in case they got lost), and sometimes, as children do, they quarrelled. But always they fell in again very quickly, and really were the very best of friends.

One day, quite suddenly, and for no reason that anyone could tell, young Paul fell ill. The only person who could be sent to fetch a doctor was the woodcutter, and he was a very old man who walked with the aid of a stick which he had cut from one of the ancient pine-trees. He took a horse from the stable, wrapped some food in an old tablecloth, and set out for the nearest town, which was said to be over a hundred miles away.

Days passed with no sign of the doctor, and the boy became more and more ill. Tess was very unhappy as she had no one to play with, and would sit all day at his bedside, chattering to him about all sorts of things to cheer him up. And always when she left him he would say: 'Please come again tomorrow, Tess.' And always, as soon as the first thrush began to sing at dawn, she would return to keep him company. Then one night, when she was saying goodbye to him, he suddenly looked very sad; and instead of the usual 'Please come again', he said: 'Tess, you are my best friend in all the world. One day I will see you in the Kingdom of Dreams.'

Now although Tess was a very bright girl for her age she was not terribly wise, and didn't know what to make of this. The more she thought about it, the more puzzled she became. She asked her parents what it could mean, but they didn't know either. In her bed that night she fell asleep still wondering at the strange thing Paul had said to her.

That same evening Paul's parents began to fear that something had happened to the old woodcutter, and at last his father decided to set out himself in search of a doctor . . . .

Paul lay awake watching the stars moving across his window, until all the creatures of the forest were silent and everyone in the house was fast asleep. He crept from his bed and stood for some time at the window, watching the moon rise until its pale light made the tree-tops shine like pure silver; until it stood, full and bright, above the topmost branch of the tallest pine-tree. Suddenly he heard a voice calling to him. At first it was very faint, and he wondered if he had only imagined someone was calling. Then it became louder, and he knew he was not mistaken.

It was a kindly voice: a voice like no other he

had ever heard. He said to himself: 'It must belong to an angel in heaven.'

The voice called to him again from the night: 'Paul! Paul!'

Paul answered: 'I am here. I am listening. What do you want?'

The angel replied: 'I have come to guide you to the Kingdom of Dreams.'

Then he noticed a silver stairway leading from his window to the ground, and heard the angel saying: 'Hurry, please hurry! I cannot wait much longer, the moon is dying . . . ' Then his feet were on the stairs and he felt the touch of guiding fingers on his arm. At the same time he thought he heard the rustle of wings; but perhaps it was a breeze stirring amongst the leaves.

With the kind angel guiding his steps he went deeper and deeper into the forest. Then all at once he remembered Tess.

'Please stop for a moment,' he begged the angel. 'Oh, please stop!'

But the angel urged him on, saying: 'We are already late. Soon the gates of the Kingdom will be

closed. Look! The moon will soon disappear.'

Paul looked up and saw that the moon had turned from silver to gold and lay half buried in a bank of cloud. In desperation he said to the angel: 'I must go back! I must!'

'But we are almost there!' cried the angel, 'and when dawn breaks I shall be spirited away, and you will be lost. You must hurry!' But even as she spoke the angel caught sight of the tear upon the boy's cheek, and her heart softened. 'What is it?' she asked him. 'Why are you crying?'

'Because,' Paul said, 'when Tess wakes and finds me gone she will be very unhappy. And I am to blame, because I left without saying goodbye to her.'

'But there is so little time,' replied the angel. 'We cannot go back now. However, I promise that if you follow me and trust me I will see what can be done, for it is clear to me that you are very fond of this girl.'

Wiping away another tear, Paul said: 'Yes, I will trust you, because I know you are good and kind, and will do your best for me.'

By this time they had arrived in a great clearing over which the last rays of the dying moon were spread like a silver fan; and there, in one corner, glinting with all the colours of an enormous rainbow, shone the gates of the great kingdom which lies beyond sleep; and, some say, beyond death: the Kingdom of Dreams. The gates were wide open, but scarcely had the travellers stepped between them than they rolled shut with a sound like thunder.

'I must leave now,' said the angel, 'but I will not forget my promise. In the morning, after you have slept, we shall see what can be done.'

Paul slept very deeply and without having a single dream, which some might think odd, considering where he was. When finally he awoke he found himself in a garden, lying on a grassy couch amongst millions of daisies and buttercups. Great banks of flowers were all around, flowers of every imaginable colour, and fountains playing.

'This place,' he thought, 'is far more beautiful than anything I have ever seen or dreamt of.'

On the grassy slopes were hundreds of young

children like himself, all laughing and playing happily together. Occasionally one would break away from the rest and come running towards him, smiling at him and beckoning him to come and join in their games. But he shook his head to all their invitations, saying to himself: 'How can I join in their games when I am not truly happy?' Then he whispered softly: 'Oh, Tess, Tess, how could I leave you without saying goodbye? And can you believe me when I say that none of the girls here is half as pretty as you?'

At that moment, as if someone had commanded him to do so, he got up and walked across a great wide lawn, then up some steps to an enormous doorway with stone columns on either side set into stone walls clothed in dark green ivy. Through this doorway he went, and on over floors of pure white marble, until he came into a great circular room, on the far side of which was a door of solid gold. As he walked slowly towards the door it swung back. Then he heard his name called in an old man's voice.

'Paul?'

'Yes,' Paul replied, 'I am here.'

The voice went on: 'You are here because I have wished it. Please enter, for I have something important to say to you.'

Paul moved inside the doorway and found himself looking into the kindly grey eyes of an old man with white hair and a white beard. He was sitting on cushions of purple velvet, in a huge chair with arms inlaid with gold and decorated with all sorts of precious stones: rubies, diamonds, amethysts and many others.

Paul thought: 'He must be the king of this land, even though he doesn't wear a crown.'

'I have been told about your unhappiness,' said the king, 'and the reason for it.'

He went on to tell Paul about the Kingdom, and how, although thousands of children came there and were happy, occasionally one was admitted whose love for someone left behind could not be forgotten.

'You are on of these,' he said to Paul, 'for your love of Tess has survived the great journey into this land.'

He looked at the boy standing before him, and his eyes were full of kindness and pity. Then he said:

'Before I tell you what has been decided, I would like you to know that the laws we live by are made by someone far greater than ourselves. On Earth this great being is known as God, whereas in the Kingdom of Dreams he is called The Great Spirit . . . but that is not important. There is only one law under which a person may be allowed to return to the place of his birth, and this law states that anyone wishing to make such a journey must forfeit – (here the old man paused and leaned forward) – his sight,' he added in what was almost a whisper.

Paul spoke without the slightest hesitation. 'I must go back,' he said, 'and whatever the price is, I will pay it.'

'Then you must make ready to leave tonight,' the king told him. 'I will set the star Venus to guide you, and you will arrive on the edge of the forest when the full moon stands clear above the tallest of the pines.'

After receiving the old king's blessing and wishes of good luck for the journey, Paul walked back to the sunlit garden with his heart full of joy and hope.

Everything happened just as the old king had said, and once again Paul found himself on the edge of the forest.

He looked across at the house where Tess lived. Reflected in her bedroom window was the full yellow disc of the moon, and below it the topmost branch of the tallest of the straight pines, pointing upward like the tip of a black arrow. He looked towards his own home for a long moment. He wished he could go there and comfort his parents, but he remembered the warning he had been given – that he must not stray from his mission for any reason at all – and he spirited himself through the dark window to the girl's bedside.

Tess was lying with one cheek pressed against her pillow and the other lit by a shaft of pale light from the moon. Paul saw that the pillow was wet and knew that she had been crying.

'Tess,' he whispered softly, 'Tess, I am here. I have come back.'

The girl stirred in her sleep. Her eyelids flickered a little, but did not open.

He bent over her and touched her cheek lightly with the tips of his fingers. Then he called to her again, and this time the sound of his voice wakened her.

'Paul?' His name was a question on her lips, and her eyes were wide with wonder. 'No, it can't be – ' She shook her head in disbelief. 'I must be dreaming . . . . '

'I came to tell you I am sorry,' he said gravely.

'Sorry?' she whispered, her eyes dark with bewilderment. 'I don't understand – '

'For leaving you like I did . . . without saying goodbye,' he explained.

He moved forward, and taking her hands in his, kissed her lightly on the cheek.

She smiled suddenly at this (for it was something he had never done before), and passed a hand over the place where she had felt the kiss.

'I came to say goodbye,' he said gently, 'and now that it is done I must go.'

Tess had been able to see him very clearly in spite of the darkness, but now he was fading slowly before her eyes.

'Oh, no!' she cried. 'No, you cannot go! You cannot leave me!'

She leapt from her bed. Her eyes were bright like new stars, and her hair flowed like dark rivers down her shoulders as she ran across the room. Through the window Paul could see the full moon slowly leaving the place where it had paused above the great pine-tree, and he heard the agitated voice of one of the Kingdom's messengers calling to him to hurry. With the silver stairway shining under his feet he turned and looked back for the last time. Tess was at the window, still holding out her arms and calling to him.

Standing once more inside the gates of the Kingdom, he knew that he could live happily in that land after all, knowing that in saying goodbye to Tess he had achieved his dearest wish. Then he remembered the forfeit.

As his sight slowly faded he walked round the garden saying goodbye in his heart to the flowers and the leaping fountains . . . and the happy children whose faces he would not see again until the end of time. Then, just as the last speck of light vanished, leaving him completely blind, he became aware of a great commotion all around him. Several times he heard his name called, now from one side, now from the other, and he wondered what it could mean.

The voices continued for some time. Then he became aware of hands reaching out from all sides and taking hold of him. They were small hands – the hands of children; and they guided him gently along pathways and down steps until the noise of birdsong and fountains disappeared, and he knew by the smell of the cool air and the stillness all around him that he was back in the great palace where he had met the old man. He stood quite still when the children left him; and he was not surprised when the next thing he heard was the familiar voice of the king.

'In our Kingdom,' he was saying, 'everything is

the opposite of what it is upon Earth. Their death is our life, and their grief is our happiness.' He paused, and Paul knew that the kindly old eyes were fixed on him. Then the king said: 'I have some good news for you, Paul. It is not often that such things happen, for miracles are as rare here as upon Earth.' He leaned forward and put a hand on Paul's shoulder. 'I have been told,' he added, 'that Tess is coming.'

Happy beyond words, Paul fell to his knees before the old man.

'You must not thank me,' said the king, 'for this is not my doing. To bring Tess here is far beyond my power. No, if anyone has made this thing possible, it can only be The Great Spirit himself – but that is not all,' he went on quickly. 'When Tess arrives in the garden – and it will be very soon now – everything must be done to make her happy; and because she cannot be made to feel responsible for your blindness, your sight will be restored to you so that you can meet her here just as you did in the country of your birth.'

Immediately Paul became aware of a strange

glow like dawn. First he saw the old man's hands spread out in front of his eyes, then the kindly face and snow-white beard.

He could see again.

'I know your tears are those of happiness,' said the king gently, 'but you must dry them just the same, for I am sure you would not want Tess to see you like this.' Then he turned in his chair and pointed towards a great door which Paul could not remember being there before. At the old man's command he stepped through it – and found himself in a long corridor. This he followed for some distance until he came to another door.

On this door, in letters of shining silver, was just one word:

REUNION

Within moments it had swung back to reveal a courtyard paved with white marble, on the far side of which, by a stone column overgrown with dark green ivy, stood Tess. She was wearing an ankle-length gown of pure white edged with green lace, and woven into her hair was a garland of white flowers.

The moment Paul stepped through the door she began to move towards him. He found himself walking, then running to meet her. Within seconds they had flung themselves into each other's arms and were spinning round and round in the sheer happiness of being together again.

In that faraway, nameless country the story is still told . . . of a young girl and boy who walk hand in hand along the old paths, through a silent forest when the full moon stands high above the topmost branch of the tallest pine-tree. It is the story of Paul and Tess, two childhood friends who found happiness together in the Kingdom of Dreams, that enchanted land where no one ever grows old, and where love lasts until the end of time.